Market Day

LIBRARIES
LEABHARLANNA

CORK CITY COUNCIL | COMHAIRLE CATHRACH CHORCAÍ

You can renew items through the online catalogue at
www.corkcitylibraries.ie, or by telephone.
Please return this item on time as others may be waiting for it.
Overdue charges: 50c per notice +5c per week.

Is féidir iasachtaí a athnuachan trí bhíthin na catalóige ag
www.corkcitylibraries.ie, nó ar an nguthán.
Muna gcuirtear iasacht ar ais in am, gearrfar costaisí
50c do gach fógra, maraon le 5c in aghaidh na seachtaine.

Class no. / Ur. aicme: _____

Scholastic Children's Books,
Commonwealth House,
1-19 New Oxford Street, London WC1A 1NU
A division of Scholastic Limited
London – New York – Toronto – Sydney – Auckland

First published in the UK by Scholastic Ltd 1989
This edition published 1996

Text copyright © John Cunliffe 1989
Illustrations copyright © Scholastic Publications Ltd and Woodland
Animations Ltd, 1989

A longer version of this story has been previously published
as a Handy Hippo.

ISBN 0 590 54142 0

Printed in Italy by LEGO S.p.a

10 9 8 7 6 5 4 3 2

John Cunliffe has asserted his moral right to be identified as
the author of the work in accordance with the Copyright, Designs
and Patents Act, 1988.

"Look at that," said Pat.

> PENCASTER AUCTION MARKET LIMITED
> ANNUAL PRIZE SHOW AND SALE –
> SATURDAY 20TH SEPTEMBER
> AT 10.30 A.M.
>
> All classes of lambs, cattle and poultry.
> Cows, goats, and pigs.

"It's years and years since I went to the show."

"Why don't you go?" said Mrs Goggins.

"I bet young Julian would like it," said Pat. "He's never been to a cattle market."

That Saturday, they all caught the Greendale bus at half-past twelve.

When they got to Pencaster, Pat said, "We'll be off to the show, then."

"I haven't time for the show," said Sara. "Somebody has to do the shopping, you know."

"We'd better come and help," said Pat.

"There isn't all that much shopping," said Sara. "I can manage. We'll meet for a cup of tea at five, in time for the six o'clock bus."

It was a long walk to the cattle-market.
It was crowded with farmers and their
wives, and there were hundreds of sheep,
and cows, bullocks, pigs, and goats, geese,
and hens.

"What a pong!" said Julian.

"And what a noise!" said Pat.

Everywhere, people were buying and
selling.

There was a space in the middle, a bit like a circus-ring, where the animals were brought to be sold. All round the ring were galleries where the people stood.

Above the ring, there was a special box where there was the most important man at the market; the auctioneer. He stood up there, at a little desk, with a wooden hammer in his hand, and looked down on everybody.

He announced each animal as it came into the ring, in a loud voice. He said who was selling it, how heavy it was, and how old it was.

Then he banged his hammer on the desk, and looked round at everyone.

"Come along now, ladies and gentlemen," he said, "who'll start us off? What am I bid?

"Shall I say a hundred-and-sixty? Who'll give me a hundred-and-sixty? One-sixty? Thank you, sir! One-sixty? Seventy? Eighty - eighty - eighty-five...; who'll say ninety? One hundred-and-ninety pounds for this fine sow? Thank you, madam. Ninety-five, ...**two hundred**...yes? Thank you! Two hundred? Any more bids? Two hundred? Going at two hundred to the lady over there! Going for the first time!" (Bang with the hammer.) "Going for the second time!" (Bang with the hammer.) "Going for the third time!" (A last bang with the hammer.) "Sold to Mrs Cowan at two hundred pounds. And next..." and off he was again.

Julian was in a muddle. How did he know that Mrs Cowan wanted that pig? She hadn't said anything at all.

All she had done was to nod and smile. Julian thought it was a funny way to spend two hundred pounds. Some people seemed to give the auctioneer a little wave when they wanted to buy something, or just touched their cap or hat.

"Look," said Pat. "There's Miss Hubbard in her new hat. She's come to see the market between bus-trips. Give her a wave. Hello, Miss Hubbard!"

Pat waved, and the auctioneer said, "Thank you, Sir, one-fifty, and...two hundred over there..."
But Pat was so busy admiring Miss Hubbard's hat that he didn't seem to notice what the auctioneer was saying.

"Dad," said Julian, "I think..."

But the auctioneer was off again, and Pat couldn't hear Julian.

Then Pat spotted Alf Thompson.
"He must have come to buy some lambs," said Pat.
"Alf! Hello, there!"
" Dad...?" said Julian.

"Fifty," said the auctioneer, "and a bargain at the price. Any more bids? Going, going, going, **gone** ..... at fifty pounds, to the gentleman with the blue scarf."

"That's you dad," said Julian.

"What?" said Pat.

"You've bought a goat. You're the man in the blue scarf."

"A goat?" said Pat. "I haven't! I haven't bought anything."

"You were waving at Alf, and that auctioneer-man thought you were waving to say you wanted to buy that goat."

"A goat?" said Pat. "Oh, dear, how much was it?"

"Fifty pounds," said Julian. "That's what he said."

"Oh dear," said Pat. "What a muddle. Whatever shall we do?"

"It's a very nice goat," said Julian.

"It might well be a very nice goat, but what are we going to do with a goat?" said Pat.

"We could milk it," said Julian. "I love goat's milk, and so does mum."

"Does she?" said Pat.

"Yes," said Julian, "and it would keep the grass short in the garden. It'd save you having to cut it."

"It'll keep the flowers short as well," said Pat.

By now, the auctioneer's helpers had come to take Pat's address. And one of them was saying, "Could you collect by 6 p.m. Sir? Pen number twenty-three."

"Er...yes," said Pat.

"And take this slip to the office, with your payment."

"Thank you," said Pat.

So this is how Pat and Julian came to be
walking through the middle of Pencaster on
Saturday afternoon, with a very lively goat,
using a length of binder-twine as a lead. A
frisky goat in an empty field is bad enough.
In the middle of Pencaster it was something
that Pat would never ever forget! The goat
was surprisingly strong. It pulled Pat this
way and that way, any way except the way
he wanted to go.

It tried to butt people. It went nosing under market-stalls to nibble at dropped vegetables and fruit. It tried to get into a supermarket. It wanted to fight dogs and cats. It knocked over a box of apples.

When Sara saw it she nearly had a fit.

"What in the world are you doing with a goat? " she said.

"We've bought it," said Julian.

"*Bought it?*" said Sara.

"It was an accident," said Pat.

"An accident?" said Sara. "How can you...?"

"He nodded," said Julian.

"Nodded?" said Sara.

"And waved."

"No!" said Sara.

"He did," said Julian. "And the man thought..."

"Which man?" said Sara.

"The auctioneer-man..."

"Oh, yes…"

"He thought dad wanted to buy the goat," said Julian.

"Oh," said Sara, "and what in the world are we going to do with a goat? And where are we going to keep it?"

"We could milk it," said Julian. "Goat's milk. Delicious."

"I love goat's milk," said Sara.

"And we could keep it in the garden," said Pat.

"It'll eat the flowers," said Sara. "But we could fence a bit of grass off for it, or even put it in Alf's field, I'm sure he wouldn't mind, specially if we gave them some of the milk. You tether them to a post."

"Brilliant," said Pat.

"We could make cheese and sell it to the visitors in summer," said Julian.

"That's a good idea," said Sara, "but how are we going to get it home?"

"I was wondering about that," said Pat.

"We could put it on the bus," said Julian. "In the luggage-space under the stairs."

"A goat on a bus?" said Sara. "I don't think Miss Hubbard would be too pleased about that. What if it eats one of those lovely seat-covers? Goats eat all kinds of things, you know."

When the bus came it was quite full, and the luggage-space under the stairs was already filled with four baskets of clucking hens. They could see at once that it wouldn't do to squeeze a goat in as well; not this goat, anyway!

"You get on the bus," said Pat, "and I'll walk the goat home."

There seemed to be no other way of getting that goat home, so Pat set out along the road, with the goat trotting alongside him. Sara and Julian waved to him as they went by in the bus. Poor Pat! It was not easy, walking with that goat. It was almost as bad in the country as it was in the town. Whenever there was a side-road, the goat wanted to go up it. Whenever there were sheep or cows in the fields, the goat wanted to be over the wall to go and play with them.

What a lucky thing it was that Ted Glen came along in his Land-rover. Ted stopped to pick Pat up as soon as he saw him. They had a struggle to get that goat in, but they did it in the end, and were soon bowling along the road home.

"My goodness," said Pat, "I *was* glad to see you. I was getting really tired of walking with that creature."

Pat got the goat home in the end, and later on Ted came back with some fencing-wire and helped him to make it a paddock at the end of the garden. Peter Fogg turned up that night with an old hen-hut on the trailer.

"We're not using this," he said, "and it'll make a snug home for your goat."